S. ... CRAMENTO PUBLIC ...

D0149448

A
DOG'S
DAY

I AM
JAX,
PROTECTOR OF
THE RANCH

I AM
JAX,
PROTECTOR OF
THE RANCH

Catherine Stier

illustrated by
Francesca Rosa

Albert Whitman & Company
Chicago, Illinois

To Raymond and Norma Stier,
with lots of love and thanks—CS

To my lovely and furry Milù—FR

Library of Congress Cataloging-in-Publication data
is on file with the publisher.
Text copyright © 2020 by Catherine Stier
Illustrations copyright © 2020 by Albert Whitman & Company
Illustrations by Francesca Rosa
First published in the United States of America
in 2020 by Albert Whitman & Company
ISBN 978-0-8075-1663-8 (hardcover)
ISBN 978-0-8075-1667-6 (ebook)
All rights reserved. No part of this book may be reproduced or transmitted
in any form or by any means, electronic or mechanical, including
photocopying, recording, or by any information storage and retrieval
system, without permission in writing from the publisher.

Printed in the United States of America
10 9 8 7 6 5 4 3 2 1 LB 24 23 22 21 20

Design by Rick DeMonico

For more information about Albert Whitman & Company,
visit our website at www.albertwhitman.com.

Contents

1. Home on the Ranch 1

2. Our Team 11

3. Danger on the Prowl 20

4. In Charge 29

5. Life of a Pup 36

6. Clover 45

7. Suspicious Scent 52

8. A New Threat 59

9. A Desperate Challenge 67

10. A New Day 76

About Livestock Guardian Dogs 86

Acknowledgments 89

Chapter 1

Home on the Ranch

I am dozing in sweet prairie grass when I see it: a quick flash of black and white fur streaks past me.

I jerk my head up from my paws.

What in thunder...

Then I settle myself. I know who that is. There's no mistaking that lightning-fast blur of energy—that's Sweep, another working dog on this ranch. Sweep and I don't hang out much, but I guess we respect each other well enough. Like me, Sweep tends to the sheep, but our jobs are very different.

My name is Jax. I'm a Great Pyrenees, but my job title is livestock guardian dog. That's what I've heard Gail, the human ranch owner, tell visitors. Like the other guardian dogs on this ranch, I rest a lot during the day. Mostly, I nap close by the sheep I guard. I may look slow next to Sweep. But when there's a predator—any animal that aims to make a meal of my sheep—I'm as quick as I need to be.

Sweep, on the other paw, is a border collie. She's a herding dog and works as a team with Gail. Together, they move the sheep from one side of the ranch to another.

Whenever Sweep shows up, I know it's time for the sheep—and me—to get a move on.

Slowly, I raise my big, furry body and stretch.

Gail gives me a pat as she walks past in her boots and big hat.

Then I feel two smaller hands ruffle my fur.

"Hey there, Jax. Did you miss me?"

I'd know that voice, that smell anywhere. It's Colton, a young human. He must be visiting the ranch today. Colton buries his face in my thick white fur and gives me a squeeze. Colton

is great kid, always kind and friendly. I might not put up with anything from predators, but Colton can hug me all he wants. I don't mind.

"Grandma, can Jax stay with us at the house tonight?" Colton asks. "Please? I bet he'd like to watch a dog movie with me."

"Grandma" is one of Gail's names, but only Colton calls her that.

Gail shakes her head. "I know Jax is a sweetheart, Colton. And I know he's your favorite. But that gentle giant wouldn't be happy in the house when his flock is out here," she says. "Those sheep are his real family. He needs to be with them and the other guardian dogs. You know that."

Colton sighs and gives me one more hug. I nuzzle my head against his shoulder to show that I like him too.

After Colton lets go of me, something on the ground catches my eye. I know I must act fast! I give Colton a firm nudge, and he stumbles back.

"Don't be so pushy, Jax," Colton says and laughs. He thinks I'm being playful. I'm not! I've just spotted a mound of dirt swarming with fire ants. One of us must have accidentally stepped on their nest. Colton may not know it, but I just saved him from some very painful ant bites.

Even though he's not one of my sheep, I watch out for Colton and my other human friends too.

"Let's move back, Colton," I hear Gail call out. "Time for Sweep to get to work."

Colton brushes off his jeans and strides away. I follow. We both know it's best to hightail it out of Sweep's way when she's on duty.

Back near the sheep, Sweep's furry face and dark ears are turned upward, tense and waiting. Finally, Gail speaks a command.

"Away to me," Gail says. Sweep silently circles to the back of the flock. After another command from Gail, Sweep drops down with her backside in the air, her head low to the ground. She aims her steady eyes at the sheep, and they skitter away from her, moving like a big fluffy cloud with hooves.

Now, if any *other* animal bossed my sheep

around that way, I'd be after that varmint. But Sweep and I have an understanding. Sweep never nips the sheep or gets too close. In her own way, she protects the sheep too, by bringing them to new feeding pastures or safer parts of the ranch.

At last, Sweep herds the flock to the fenced-in pasture where they'll stay for the night. I trot along behind.

With her work done, Sweep bounds alongside Colton and Gail through the pasture gate. They hop into Gail's big white pickup truck and rumble away.

Sweep will probably spend tonight in a soft doggy bed in Gail's ranch house. But me? I am glad to stay right here, where I am needed.

I may sleep during the day, but I'm busy and extra alert at night. Dusk to dawn is the most

dangerous time for my flock. There are things in the dark that terrify sheep—with good reason. Just yesterday, in the dead of the night, I heard some high-pitched howls a ways off.

That has me worried.

So now, as the sun sets and the humans and the herding dog wind down their day, *my* workday begins.

Chapter 2
Our Team

With so many sheep to watch over, I'm glad I'm not the only one on guard duty.

Bev, our lead guardian dog, is here too. Bev is an Anatolian shepherd by breed, with a light-brown coat and a curling tail. She's the oldest dog on the ranch. I've learned a lot by watching her. Still, Bev has a different style than me. She likes to stay close to our flock unless there's trouble to chase away.

Then there's Stormy, the tough, guardian-pup-in-training. She's a Great Pyrenees, like me. At just over a year old, she still stays close to Bev. I worry about Stormy a bit. Young pups make mistakes sometimes, mistakes that can be painful to themselves or dangerous for the sheep. I know. I made mistakes when I was a youngster.

And me? I'm the wanderer of our trio. It's my job to jog along the fence, patrolling the edges of the pasture.

It's our differences that make us such a great team.

Even though we tackle our guard work in our own ways, we three dogs have a lot in common. We are big dogs, about as tall as the sheep we watch over. Dogs like us don't need to spend much time with a human trainer to become good at our jobs. We have something better—what Gail calls our *instincts*. Guarding those in our animal and human families comes naturally to us.

Now that I'm wide-awake, I move to the far side of the pasture. The fenced-in area is long and wide—bigger than the barn, the ranch house, and the horse stable all put together.

That's a lot of ground to cover. I keep my eyes open and sniff the many scents in the air. I search for anything that might be bad news for my sheep. Now and then, I send out a warning.

Wwwoof.

Wwwoof.

That's just to let any crafty critters know I'm on the job.

The sheep don't pay any mind to my barking. They're used to it. The flock still grazes and

moves about. When the sun disappears, they will rest. Some of the ewes—that's what Gail calls the female sheep that make up my flock—will nestle down in the grass.

Just ahead by the fence, I see movement. My muscles tense. But then I relax. It's only a doe with her fawn. They are coming out to feed at twilight. I pause, and the tiny fawn looks at me with dark eyes.

We've met before. The mama deer isn't afraid of me. She's not a threat to my sheep, so she knows I won't bother her. That mama deer knows, too, that this pasture is safer than the woods. I help keep away hungry animals that might attack her baby.

I jog farther along the fence. The night is warm. A fading yellow sunset lights the wide Texas sky. I stop now and then to lift my leg and wet the ground, the way dogs do. This bit of scent is my Keep Out sign for foxes, coyotes, and other animals. Those thin, wily critters have no problem slipping through the pasture fence. Usually, the sight of us dogs and the scent markers we leave are enough to keep dangerous animals away.

But not always.

Still, all seems peaceful on the ranch tonight.

As the final colors of the sunset fade, the moon comes out.

Uh-oh.

It's a *full* moon tonight. Strange things seem to happen when the moon is full. We see more predators. Animals act up in unexpected ways.

The sky grows darker. I keep moving along the pasture fence and send out more warning barks.

Wwwoof.

Wwwoof.

I gaze around and sniff and leave more scent markers. I am at the far end of the pasture, a long way from my sheep and the other dogs, when something changes.

Something that makes me think about the spine-chilling howls I heard the night before.

And then I know—this will be no ordinary night.

Far off by the sheep, I see our lead dog, Bev. She faces the woods. From the way she stands and stares, I can tell that Bev senses something—some kind of danger.

I follow Bev's gaze. There, behind the fence

at the woods' edge, I spot it—a dark shape creeping forward. The shape moves into the moonlight. Even from here, I can see a shaggy body and long, thin legs. I see dark fur and pointed ears.

A coyote!

Chapter 3

Danger on the Prowl

In a blink, the skinny coyote slips through the fence. It trots through the high grass. It eyes our sheep and watches Bev.

Most coyotes are too smart to get near our flock. They find out quickly that we guardian dogs will protect our sheep with our lives.

But coyotes like meat, and they look for easy meals. They'll sometimes prey on large animals. Mostly, they seek out the small or weak.

I think about the young sheep in our flock.

That part deep inside of me called instinct blazes to life. No coyote is going to mess with those I protect! I take off from the far end of the pasture to join Bev.

As I sprint, the commotion begins. All the sheep are up and moving. They have a good sense of smell—and now they smell coyote. Some of the sheep wear bells on their necks. A noisy clanging rings out through the pasture as the scared sheep move into a tight circle. They stamp their feet and snort.

I hear Bev give a warning growl that grows into a bark. The sound is deep and loud. Bev and I are each at least three times the weight of a coyote. But the shaggy coyote keeps slinking toward our flock. Maybe it's extra bold—or extra hungry.

Bev moves forward, barking loudly. Suddenly two more coyotes slip through the fence! A single coyote is bad enough. A group of coyotes is much more dangerous. They can work together, with one chasing prey right into the jaws of another. Or they can surround a lone guardian dog.

The three coyotes pace back and forth. They eye one of the smaller ewes.

I am running and barking with all my might. Little Stormy runs on her puppy legs to get to Bev too.

We are not fast enough. Even with all of our warning barks, the coyotes don't back down. Bev has no choice. She must face the three coyotes on her own.

Bev springs forward. The coyotes stop creeping toward the sheep, and jerk their heads up. Stormy and I run and bark, but Bev is still far ahead of us.

As Bev closes in, two of the coyotes turn and run from the pasture. They dive through the fence and head for the woods.

But not the shaggiest coyote. It stays and bares its teeth. It lunges at Bev and then jumps back. I hear Bev yelp with surprise. Has she been bitten? Clawed? Things are happening so fast, I'm not sure. But Bev is still ready to fight. She bolts after the coyote, nearly catching its back leg. The coyote is both lucky and quick. It turns and runs away, fast as a prairie fire.

By the time Stormy and I reach Bev, the would-be sheep thief is gone. Like the other coyotes, it darts through the fence and disappears into the dark woods. The last we see is the tip of its tail as it crashes through the brush. With Bev on the job, it's a wonder that the coyote still *has* a tail. Bev faces the woods and barks. I see up close the gash on her face.

We dogs move back, closer to the herd. All three of us are panting. The sheep still move about. I know they'll be restless for a while.

In the ranch house down the way, the lights are on. Gail must have heard the racket. Soon her big white truck is rumbling down the road. It stops near where our sheep huddle together.

Gail aims the truck's headlights at the flock. The sheep's eyes glow in the headlights' beams. The sheep are all safe, even the lambs.

Gail jumps from the truck and yanks open the gate. She looks to the woods. We hear coyote yips and howls a ways off. The sounds echo through the night.

"Seems the predators are on the prowl," Gail says. "Did y'all chase off a coyote tonight?"

Not just one coyote, I think. *Three hungry beasts!*

Gail gives each of us a pat.

"Good job, Jax," she says. "Atta girl, Stormy."

Then she spots the slash on Bev's muzzle.

"Poor girl," Gail says. She runs her hands along Bev's back and tummy, looking for other injuries. "Don't you worry about that nasty cut," Gail says in a soothing voice. "You know I take good care of my crew, Bev. You've got everything from your rabies shot to your rattlesnake vaccine. I expect you'll be fine. But let's get you to the vet just to be sure."

Gail puts a leash on Bev's collar and brings her to the truck. I can see a sleepy Colton waiting, his face pressed to the back-seat window. Colton's eyes grow wide as Gail leads the bleeding Bev through the gate.

"Let's see if Doc Lopez can see one more patient at this late hour," Gail says to Colton as she helps Bev into the truck.

The motor starts, and Gail's truck cruises away. It heads down the road toward town.

I know Gail will take good care of Bev. With Colton along, Bev will surely get an extra dose of loving too.

But now I am the oldest dog in this pasture.

I am in charge.

There's a full moon.

And Gail and her big truck won't be around if there's any more trouble tonight.

Chapter 4

In Charge

Don't get me wrong. I'm a dog who likes excitement. But I've got a lot to keep track of tonight. Our lead dog is gone. I have a puppy to watch over. And there's that full moon lighting up the pasture.

I hope that full moon doesn't mean *more* trouble.

Without Bev around, Stormy sticks close to me. She learns from watching us bigger dogs, I

know. I can show her what a guardian dog does to protect a flock. I can model the right way to act. But there are some things I can't warn Stormy about. Things I learned the hard way as a puppy.

We guardian dogs can usually tell what is and is not a threat. But as a pup, I ran into a plump, wild creature I had never seen before. It had small eyes and strange, sticky-up hair. It wandered under the fence and into the pasture early one evening.

Porcupines do not eat sheep. I know that now. But as a pup—well, I went after the intruder. And you guessed it—I ended up with face full of quills. The porcupine just waddled away under the fence. It was fine. I was not! Those quills hurt like crazy!

I remember lying with my nose in Gail's lap. She spoke soft words as she pulled out each quill.

"Be brave, Jax," she said. "I'll have these out in no time. It's a hard lesson to learn. But I bet you never tangle with that old porcupine again."

I whined and whimpered. But I survived. And Gail was right. I learned my lesson.

I hope that is a lesson Stormy never has to learn.

There are other things to keep watch for tonight too.

A big ewe moves away from the flock. Her belly is low, and she walks slowly in my direction. This she-sheep stops before me a moment. Then she turns and leads me away. I follow. She heads to a spot under the juniper tree, away from the others. The big ewe lies down. I understand my sheep well enough to know what this means. This sheep is about to have a baby!

This is a dangerous time for both the mama sheep and her soon-to-arrive lamb. A sheep in labor can't run from predators. And a newborn lamb can hardly stand at first.

I don't stare at the ewe. Something inside me knows that might make her nervous. Instead, I turn my back and guard her as she gets ready to deliver her lamb. Somehow, I just know it's the right thing to do. Still, I worry about the rest of the flock. I am not far from the other sheep. But I am not running and checking the pasture edges like I usually do. A predator could sneak in, and I might not know until it's too late.

Stormy has followed me. She's curious about what's happening with the ewe. She edges forward.

I step between the ewe and Stormy, hoping the pup gets the hint. That mama ewe doesn't need Stormy's help.

I guess Stormy is growing up though. Maybe her own instincts are kicking in. The tough pup knows it's best to leave my side now. She knows

the rest of the flock needs protection too. I am relieved when Stormy turns and moves closer to the flock.

I stand in the grass and hear the low sounds of the mama sheep behind me. If all goes well, I'll meet the new little lamb tonight.

Chapter 5
Life of a Pup

I'd rather be roaming. But I stay put. I hear the ewe behind me walking, laying down, then getting up again.

I guess her little lamb is in no hurry to be born tonight. Still, I'll stand guard for as long as this sheep needs me. It's what I've been raised to do.

When I was a newborn pup, the farmer who took care of my mama tucked soft, fuzzy bits into our bedding. I found out later that it was sheep's wool. Even as I cuddled close to my mama and my brothers and sisters, I was surrounded by the smell of sheep.

Later, when I was a few weeks old, that farmer put me in a pen with a friendly young ewe. There was something familiar about the ewe, a smell I knew from the time when I could barely open my eyes. I remember nosing closer

to her. The ewe didn't mind. She looked at me and playfully nipped at my tail.

After a while, I met some lambs too. They were some of my first playmates. If I ever jostled a lamb too much, though, a mama sheep would give me a firm nudge. That was her way of saying, "Hold on there, pup. Behave yourself. You must be gentle with my little one."

Then somehow, without being told or trained, it happened—the sheep and I had bonded for life. The farmer had a word for it. "Well, Jax, looks like those sheep have imprinted on you, all right," he said once when I snuggled near two lambs, just as I once did with the other puppies in my litter. *Imprinted?* All I know is that from that time on, I would do whatever it took to keep all sheep safe from harm.

Meeting Bev was another story. When I was old enough to leave my mama, Gail brought me to her ranch. Everything at Gail's ranch was so interesting and different! Suddenly, I had new places to explore and new scents to discover.

One morning, Gail brought me on a leash to the pasture. I wanted to rush right over to meet the sheep. Instead, Gail guided me to a big dog resting in the grass.

"Bev," Gail said to the big dog. "This is Jax. He's going to help you watch over our flock. He's a bit frisky, but I bet he'll be a hard worker. Plus, you'll have some canine company out here. Well, girl, what do you think of this new pup?"

Bev stood up—and up and up. This huge dog looked down at me.

As I recall, I was a big ball of fluff then, only four months old, but I wasn't a bit afraid. I bounded forward and gave the older dog a good sniff. She was a bigger dog like my mama, but she didn't smell or look like her. Still, I hopped up and down, eager to play.

Bev lowered her head to check out my scent too. I flopped down belly-side up and batted her ear with my paw. Patient Bev nudged me with her muzzle, then looked up at Gail as if to say, "You expect me to work with this little fur ball?"

"Oh, the look on your face, Bev," Gail said, laughing. "Don't worry. Jax won't always be a pesky little puppy. He'll watch you and learn from you. With your guidance, I know he'll grow up to be a top-notch guardian dog, just like you."

Gail brought me to the pasture many more times, as she did chores and checked on the flock. She'd let me off the leash, but she kept a close eye on me. Big old Bev watched me too. A pup that chases the sheep or plays too rough is a problem, but I guess I did fine. I didn't nip at any sheep ears or bite at their wool. After many months of getting to know the flock, I joined Bev for my first whole day and night on the job. I've been learning from her ever since.

Now, I know Colton thinks I got a tough break having to work outside all night. But tonight I look around and see what Sweep and other dogs that stay inside at night are missing. There are more stars in the sky than there are wildflowers in a Texas field. Throughout the pasture, fireflies flash and glow.

Then there are the sounds. Insects buzz in the trees and chirp in the grass. Tonight, a mockingbird is singing every song he knows, one after the other.

The heat of the day is gone, and a soft breeze full of interesting smells washes past my face and ruffles my fur.

Sweep's probably sitting pretty right now on a couch in a stuffy living room. But I look around at my sheep settling down for the night. I know there's nowhere else I'd rather be.

Chapter 6

Clover

I'm listening to the songs of nature when I hear grass rustling behind me. The mama sheep is up and moving again. I turn around. In the moonlight I see a tiny wet creature lying on the ground. The baby lamb is here!

The ewe's a good mama, doing just what needs to be done for her baby. She begins licking the lamb clean. She starts first with the tiny mouth, so the little lamb can breathe freely.

I am relieved. Things went well this night for both the sheep and her baby! I know that's not always the case. Sometimes during the birth of a lamb—or *lambing* as it's called on the ranch—a sheep needs help from Gail, or even the vet. And sometimes, a mama sheep seems confused about how to care for her lamb. She won't clean it or feed it. She might even wander off from her helpless baby! But I don't worry about this pair. This sheep knows how to tend to her lamb.

After several minutes, Stormy ambles over. Again, I place my body between the curious pup and the mama with her lamb. I make sure Stormy can see them but stays away.

I am proud of the way Stormy keeps still. She doesn't bound forward to check out the new scents or this funny little newborn creature. It's a good thing too! That mama sheep would have

no patience with a rowdy pup getting anywhere near her helpless babe.

As we two dogs watch, the tiny lamb begins to wriggle about. Her long, thin legs tangle as she struggles upward. After a tumble or two back onto the soft grass, she's finally up, standing on her own little hooves. Bits of dried grass and clover stick to the lamb's wet wool. Clover, I think, would be a good name for this lamb.

Clover takes a few awkward steps toward

the ewe. She ducks under her mama and begins feeding. She fills up with the warm milk her little body needs to grow strong. Like her mama, Clover knows instinctively what to do. This tells me this lamb is strong and healthy.

After she's fed, Clover wobbles forward and gazes at us dogs. We are the first creatures she has seen, besides her mama. She isn't frightened, but doesn't seem to know what to make of us.

This time, Stormy's curiosity gets the best of her. She ignores my good example of staying back and quiet and calm. Quick as a wink, Stormy skirts around me, head up, tongue hanging from her mouth. She heads straight for the lamb, eager to say hello. I know Stormy means no harm. She just wants to check out this newest member of our flock.

But if I don't act fast, things might get ugly.

I move quickly, but the mama ewe is even quicker. As Stormy draws close, the mama lowers her head and stomps the ground. With angry eyes, the sheep charges forward.

Yelp!

Stormy cries out in surprise. She bolts back just in time to avoid a firm head-butt.

As I circle around Stormy and nudge her away from Clover, I worry. A good guardian dog knows better than to get too close to a protective ewe's lamb. Stormy made a rookie mistake. I don't think we can afford mistakes tonight.

I am depending on Stormy to help me watch over Clover and all the other sheep now that

Bev is not around. Sheep can be tough, but they don't have claws or sharp, pointy teeth. They aren't able to defend themselves against nature's biggest, baddest hunters. That's where we dogs come in.

But now the scent of a newborn lamb might draw the interest of more predators. Is Stormy too young to be a reliable guardian? Is she ready for the challenges we may face tonight? Am I?

Chapter 7
Suspicious Scent

Tonight's situation sure has me troubled. Part of me longs to do what I always do—keep the flock safe by running along the fence line. But the other part of me knows there's a newborn lamb to consider. I don't dare stray too far from Clover and her mama. When Stormy moves back to the rest of the flock, I pace back and forth a short stretch from the juniper tree.

The sheep have calmed, and many are bedded down on the grass. The coyotes, it seems, have moved on. There's plenty for coyotes to eat, like rodents or birds or rabbits. They also eat what Gail calls *carrion*, the remains of animals that have died. Some pesky coyotes will even raid garbage cans. Those three crafty coyotes are probably feasting right now.

My own stomach rumbles. I figure I'd be wise to fuel up so I have the energy I need for tonight. Luckily, nighttime snacking is not a problem. The automatic dog feeding station Gail set up is close by. It's pretty nifty, designed to let dogs in but keep out sheep, goats, and other animals.

On three sides of the dog feeding station, there's a high wire fence. At the front, Gail has put sturdy branches long-ways across the opening. They are too high for a sheep to step over, and too close together for a lamb to squeeze through. I take one last look at Clover and her mama, and then I move my gaze to the flock. All seems well. I believe I can spare a moment for some quick grub.

With a little hop and wiggle, I'm over the branches and inside the fenced walls of the feeding station. Against the back fence, Gail has attached a gray metal box chock-full of tasty dog food. I nudge the little front door open with my muzzle. Yum! The food inside is dry and fresh and ready for me to chow down on.

As I munch happily, I wonder for a moment how Bev is doing at the vet. Bev and Gail and Colton have been gone for some time. No white truck has rumbled back from town yet.

I've visited Dr. Lopez's office before. I know it takes awhile to get there on the country roads. And the Doc is a friendly type. He and Gail can talk for quite a spell when they get going, even in the middle of the night. They're probably gabbing about family and farming and the lambing season and such. *Bev is fine*, I tell myself. *She'll be back home soon.*

With my belly full, I wiggle back over the fence and have a look around. I lift my head in the direction of the woods. Something has changed. With the many scents of the night, I breathe in a separate strand of something unusual. My nose is great at bringing in and holding on to smells as my brain decodes them. And right now my brain is telling me that the strange scent can mean only one thing: *cat.*

The smell unsettles me. It's a feline scent all

right, but I can't lock in to what kind. Is there a bobcat out there, eyeing the flock from the shadows? Or is it just passing close by, looking to make a meal of the squirrels and rabbits of the forest?

I once saw a bobcat prowling at a distance. It looked like a bigger, leggier version of a barn cat, but with a speckled coat and extra fur around its face. It also had a round clump of a tail at its rump. It's rare for a bobcat to come after the sheep. But I'm beginning to feel that on a night like this, anything can happen.

Chapter 8

A New Threat

Cat isn't the only new scent. Not fair off, I smell the dusty-wet scent of rain as well. A few misty clouds drift in to the otherwise clear night sky, not quite covering the moon.

I trot to where I left the mama ewe and Clover. Clover is still tucked with her mama under the big juniper tree. If the rains do come this way, Clover should be snug under the tree's feathery, green cover.

It's not long before a few warm raindrops fall on my face. I don't feel the drops anywhere else on my body. Great Pyrenees like me have a weather resistant coat. I have a fine, soft fur layer underneath, topped with a coarse and shaggy coat on top.

The sheep are doing all right too, in their woolly covering. A light spring rain doesn't trouble us.

But something else does trouble me.

That feline scent?

It just got stronger, much stronger.

I swivel my head in the direction of the scent. At first, all I see is the solid rocky ledge rising above the pasture. Then I look up through the rain.

For just a second, I freeze. A strange shape is silhouetted on the ledge, far above my head. This long, lean animal is much bigger than any predator we've seen around here. This is no coyote. The smell of feline is strong, but this is no bobcat either. Even in the dark, my eyes can tell that this cat's fur is sleek and unmarked. The long tail nearly touches the ground.

The animal slinks silently on enormous paws along the rocky ledge, then stops and stares downward. At us. At the sheep. It is calculating its next move, I can tell.

The rocky ledge isn't far from the juniper tree that shelters Clover and her mama.

I figure out a lot in a split second. This beast is some kind of enormous wild cat, but it's not very old, I'm guessing. The paws look too big for its body, like they do on a not-quite-grown-up puppy. I reckon when it comes to hunting on its own, this cat is a greenhorn—still a bit unpracticed. That's probably why it's thinking of giving fenced-in sheep a try.

My first goal is to keep the cat up there, on the ledge—outside the pasture.

But right now, this cat has all the advantages. There's no way I could climb up that steep ledge. This big cat, though, could easily leap from its perch into the pasture.

I burst into a run and bring out my loudest, fiercest howl.

Arrrrooof. Arrrrooof.

My barking seems to have stopped it in its tracks. I bark and howl and bark and lunge. I am tense, dreading what might happen next, hoping the cat turns and runs.

But the big cat stays. It takes its time, not making any fast moves. I'm grateful for this. I'm

hoping this hesitation gives Stormy a chance to catch up with me. Maybe facing two barking dogs will make this creature think twice about invading our pasture. Still, the cat's strong muscles look ready to snap into action at any moment.

I chance a quick glance back at the flock. Stormy's at full volume, barking and dodging her way through the fleeing sheep as she runs toward me. I turn back to face the rocky ledge. I see how the cat looks over my head at the sheep, focused and agitated by their movement. I'm betting all that running is making the cat itching to pounce.

Clover and her mama, the two closest sheep, begin skittering away too. The young lamb slips on the wet ground as she struggles on her new legs to follow her mama. Clover is on the ground, helpless.

That's when the big cat leaps.

Chapter 9

A Desperate Challenge

The wild cat lands on the ground in front of me. Now I know how Bev felt, a lone dog facing a desperate predator.

I quickly turn my body so I am between the cat and the escaping Clover.

All this cat has to do is back away and leave the pasture. There's plenty out there to hunt tonight. I don't want either of us to end up hurt.

But it doesn't stop. When the big cat makes a move toward Clover, I lunge.

Everything happens so fast. The cat's paws grip me around my middle, and we twist together. In the fray, I see fangs and claws, but they miss their mark. For a moment, I pin the cat. It's strong, though. It forces its way from my hold, knocking me over.

Crash!

The cat hurtles backward, smashing into our dog feeder pen and leaving a big dent in the wire fencing. In a flash, the feline is on its feet, hissing and snarling.

I'm still on my back from the impact of the cat throwing me off. The cat's about to leap at me when Stormy catches up. I'm worried Stormy will be so excited she'll try to battle that beast on her own. I doubt Stormy would survive.

But that's not what Stormy does. Instead, that pup does something smart.

Stormy comes sideways at the cat, and it abandons the attack on me. While I jump to my feet, Stormy places herself so that the cat is trapped exactly where she wants it.

Stormy is on one side of the cat, and I'm on another. The feeding station fence is behind the cat. Stormy and I have formed a square with one side open—the side facing the rocky ledge. We are closing in. All the cat has to do is scoot out of our pasture, back up the ledge.

Instead, the cat crouches and hisses and shows its bright white teeth. It whips its head from me to Stormy to me again. When it tries to back up, its backside bangs against the feeding station.

Finally the feline gets smart. It figures we dogs are too much to tangle with tonight.

Silently and speedily, it leaps onto the rocky ledge, graceful as a barn cat. With one more leap, the scoundrel is gone.

Stormy and I keep up our barking for a while, for good measure. My insides are blazing with that high-energy fire I feel when I face a predator. But I'm mightily relieved too. Two attacks in one night, and no sheep lost. That's surely something we dogs can take pride in.

I am proud of Stormy too. She didn't just leap into the fray with the cat, like I was worried she might. That may have put her—and me and the sheep—in danger. Surrounding the cat and forcing it away worked out the best for all of us.

Maybe Stormy learned something from watching us older dogs tonight. Bev and I both held back from attacks, trying to frighten the predators away until we had no choice. Or maybe Stormy learned on her own. After all, she very nearly suffered a serious head-butt from Clover's mama when she rushed at the lamb. Either way, it's clear Stormy has proven herself to be a great guardian dog.

As for that scoundrel of a wild cat—well, I know it wasn't really a scoundrel. Just a hungry wild animal without a ranch owner to keep it well-fed. Likely, the cat grew too big to stay with its mama, and it's still learning how to hunt for itself. It probably wandered this way, seeking out a territory of its own. I don't wish that cat any ill will. It just needs to know that this here pasture can't be part of its hunting grounds. Not on my watch.

The rain doesn't last long, and things settle down. Far off, I see headlights coming down the road. It's Gail's old white truck returning home. The truck doesn't come as far as the pasture though. Gail trusts that all is well, so isn't inclined to check on us. The truck turns into the driveway of the ranch house.

Chapter 10

A New Day

The long night of the full moon finally winds down. I watch the sun nudge itself above the horizon. Light begins to flood the pasture.

Clover and her mama are resting. I reckon it's a good time to patrol the pasture again. I set off. Just outside the fence, I spot the doe and fawn. I see the mama and baby made it safely through the night too.

The morning noises fill the air as I make my rounds. Birds whistle and warble. Crickets add their chirps to the sunrise song.

It's not long before the rumble of Gail's truck draws me to the gate. Stormy makes her way over too. We know a morning visit from Gail usually means a friendly word—and sometimes a treat. Gail pulls into the pasture and slides out of the truck with Sweep at her heels. Our lead dog Bev jumps out. I'm happy to see she looks good as new. Last of all, Colton pops out of the back seat.

"Jax, you missed all the excitement," Colton says, heading straight to me. "We took Bev to the vet's and didn't get home till really late. Then Bev and I had a sleepover, right in Grandma's living room. But Bev didn't sleep much," Colton said with a yawn. "She kept walking over my sleeping bag."

"Old Bev worried about her sheep all night, didn't you, girl?" Gail says.

Stormy and I greet Bev with a good sniffing. I smell in her fur the ranch house and medicine and the vet's office. And doggy treats. Colton's been spoiling her!

Bev sniffs me closely too. She senses the big cat's scent on me. I think I see curiosity and a new respect for me and Stormy in her eyes. Coming from Bev, that means a lot.

The sheep have spotted Gail. They begin

moving toward us, expecting their breakfast.

"Hold on, girls," Gail tells the sheep. She squints out in the pasture. "Is that a new lamb I see?"

Gail heads toward the juniper tree, and Colton and us dogs follow.

"Look at you!" Gail tells Clover. "What a sturdy little lamb you are! We'll load you and your mama up in the trailer later and check you both out."

Then Gail notices the smashed-in fence of the feeding station.

"What in thunder happened here?" Gail asks. She examines the feeding station then steps back, eyeing the ground.

"Well, I'll be! Colton, come see this."

Colton rushes over as Gail crouches and points to a track in the damp dirt.

"A dog track?" Colton asks.

"There are some dog tracks here in this mud, but this—this is something different. This is the footprint of a mountain lion."

Gail turns to Stormy and me in amazement. "Jax, Stormy, did you two face down a mountain lion last night?"

So that's what that big cat was—a *mountain lion.*

I raise my head proudly.

"A mountain lion?" Colton asks.

"Or cougar, or puma. That wild cat goes by lots of names," says Gail.

"How can you tell it's a mountain lion?" Colton asks.

"A dog's footprint has marks where its nails hit the soil. But look at this one here. See how the heel is wider, almost shaped like an *M*? This was definitely a cat, and the only cat that big is a mountain lion. Judging by what happened to the feeding station, there was quite a tussle."

Gail checks Stormy and me out, looking at our faces and bellies and backs. She discovers what I already know—we weren't hurt, protected in part by our thick fur.

Satisfied that we are fine, Gail steps back and says something that makes my tail wag.

"Let's give these dogs an extra treat, Colton. They've earned it! They saved the sheep. And probably that mountain lion too."

"But they fought the mountain lion," Colton says. He hands me a biscuit.

"It appears so," Gail admits. "But if that cat made a kill in our pasture, it might get a taste for sheep meat. Going after livestock could become a habit, and it would probably start raiding other farms and ranches around here too. Then, who knows what people might do to stop it? Sometimes predators like coyotes and mountain lions have been hunted or poisoned or trapped. By running the cat off, these dogs probably convinced it to stick to hunting wild animals, like it's meant to. You've done well, my brave dogs."

As I munch on the second biscuit Colton hands me, I have to agree.

Soon, Sweep is on duty again. With a command from Gail, Sweep holds back the sheep with her steely eyes so Gail can pour their food without getting overrun by those hungry ewes. When those sheep finish their meal, Sweep will likely herd the flock back to another pasture. Then it will be time for me to move too.

Still, while I have the chance, I settle in the grass and close my eyes for a spell. Colton is next to me, stroking my fur and telling me what a good boy I am. It's like a lullaby, and soon I'm drifting off.

In my dreams I see the coyotes, returning to their den with rabbit meat for their hungry pups. I watch the young mountain lion, leaping up a hillside somewhere far from this ranch. I see Clover in my dreams too, all grown-up with lambs of her own.

And I doze happily, knowing that I have a job that suits me just fine, and one I do well.

About Livestock Guardian Dogs

For as long as people have raised livestock, they have looked for ways to protect them. As a result, livestock guardian dogs (LGDs) have been on the job for thousands of years.

Today, there are at least forty breeds of LGDs. And while all guardian dogs have similar jobs, they protect many different kinds of animals around the world, from sheep and goats and cattle to llamas and alpacas and ostriches.

LGDs come face-to-face with all kinds of predatory critters, too, including coyotes, mountain lions, cheetahs, leopards, bears, wolves—even baboons! It might seem strange, but the dogs also play an important role in protecting these animals. Wild animals that are caught preying on livestock might get in big trouble with livestock owners, who need their animals to make a living. Guardian dogs help keep wild animals in the wild and those being raised by people out of harm's way.

Livestock guardian dogs do not live inside family homes, like many dogs do. To be successful, they need to spend most of their time with the animals they protect, starting during puppyhood. At just a couple months old, LGDs start living with the members of the flock or herd they will guard, bonding with them and becoming like family. And while it's important that the dogs become comfortable working with humans and learn to obey commands, their home is in the fields, not in the house.

After about six months, livestock guardian dogs' instincts start to kick in, and they naturally start to defend the animals they've bonded with. Good guardian dogs are at home and relaxed around their livestock. But they are also great at noticing threats, and they have the strength and the smarts to protect their flock or herd.

Livestock guardian dogs have important and difficult jobs. But behind their big, tough looks, they are a lot like other dogs. They need care and attention from humans, including consistent contact with people and regular trips to the vet. And, like all dogs, they return that care and attention with loyalty and love.

🐾 LGDs in this Book 🐾

Great Pyrenees

The Great Pyrenees was bred to stop predators from attacking sheep in the snowy Pyrenees Mountains between France and Spain. Today, Pyrs are a common livestock guardian breed, but can also make great pets!

Height: 25–32 inches
Weight: 85+ pounds
Life Span: 10–12 years
Coat: All white, or white with markings of gray, tan, or red-brown
Known for: Smarts and calm

Anatolian Shepherd

The history of Anatolian shepherds goes back about 6,000 years to the mountains of Turkey. They are strong and independent and very devoted to those they protect.

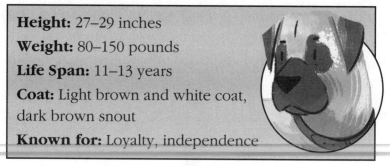

Height: 27–29 inches
Weight: 80–150 pounds
Life Span: 11–13 years
Coat: Light brown and white coat, dark brown snout
Known for: Loyalty, independence

Breed information based on American Kennel Club data.

Acknowledgments

Foremost, I'd like to thank Reid Redden, PhD, Texas AgriLife Extension Associate Professor and Sheep and Goat Specialist and a livestock guardian dog advocate, who answered my many questions and reviewed a draft of the manuscript. Dr. Redden also graciously arranged an extraordinary opportunity for me to visit his parents' ranch.

A very special thank-you to Tacy Redden, Dr. Redden's mother, who, along with her granddaughter Reece Redden, were my hosts for a tour of their lovely Texas ranch one misty morning. There I witnessed both livestock guardian dogs and a feisty herding dog at work with the sheep and goats. Both Tacy and Reece were generous with their time and shared their knowledge about the important work of guardian dogs on a ranch.

During my research on livestock guardian dogs, I found the books of author/shepherd Cat Urbigkit to be most interesting and informative, including her book *Shepherds of Coyote Rocks: Public Lands, Private Herds, and the Natural World* as well as her lively interview with Marcie Davis on the *Working Like Dogs* podcast episode #81, "Guardian Dogs and the Herds They Protect."

Finally, I was most impressed by the sheep herding skills of the amazing border collies at the San Antonio Stock and Rodeo's sheep dog trials. Three handlers who participated that day—Alexis Ender, Betty Gillis, and Art Tanguma—graciously helped enlighten me about herding dogs for this book, and allowed me to meet their talented border collies.